LITTLE SIMON

An imprint of Simon & Schuster Children's Publishing Division • 1230 Avenue of the Americas, New York, New York 10020 • First Little Simon hardcover edition February 2016 • Copyright © 2016 by Simon & Schuster, Inc. All rights reserved, including the right of reproduction in whole or in part in any form. LITTLE SIMON is a registered trademark of Simon & Schuster, Inc., and associated colophon is a trademark of Simon & Schuster, Inc. For information about special discounts for bulk purchases, please contact Simon & Schuster Special Sales at 1-866-506-1949 or business@simonandschuster.com. The Simon & Schuster Speakers Bureau can bring authors to your live event. For more information or to book an event contact the Simon & Schuster Speakers Bureau at 1-866-248-3049 or visit our website at www.simonspeakers.com. Designed by Laura Roode. The text of this book was set in Usherwood. Manufactured in the United States of America 0116 FFG
10 9 8 7 6 5 4 3 2 1
Cataloging-in-Publication Data for this title is available from the Library of Congress.
ISBN 978-1-4814-5184-0 (hc)
ISBN 978-1-4814-5183-3 (pbk)
ISBN 978-1-4814-5185-7 (eBook)

the adventures of

SOPHIE MOUSE

7

The clover curse

By Poppy Green • Illustrated by Jennifer A. Bell

LITTLE SIMON

New York London Toronto Sydney New Delhi

Contents

chapter 1

The Groundhog's Rainbow

Mrs. Wise closed the book she had just read out loud to the class. Sophie sighed. *Wow! What a story!* she thought.

A groundhog had found a hidden stairway in a tree. He'd climbed it all the way to the top branch. But the stairway kept going. So the ground-hog did too—into the clouds and over a rainbow! He found a magical world

on the other side.

Sophie loved the story and the way it was told. It didn't feel like a fairy tale. It was written as if it had really happened!

"All right class," said Mrs. Wise.

"Who can tell me what a *legend* is?"

Lydie, Hattie Frog's big sister, raised her hand.

"It's a story that animals believe in," Lydie said. "But there's no proof that it really happened."

Mrs. Wise nodded. "That's a good way to put it," she said. "Have any of you heard stories like this? Are there any legends of Silverlake Forest?"

A few hands went up around the one-room schoolhouse.

"The Tale of the Fox's Tail!" said Zoe the bluebird.

Sophie nodded. That one was about a fox whose tail would not stop growing.

"The Myth of the Mousebug!" Ben the rabbit suggested.

4

Sophie squeaked excitedly. She was fascinated by the tale of a mouse who turned into a bug! A ladybug swooped in through a classroom window. It flew around Sophie's head. Then it landed on the windowsill. Sophie stared at the bug as her mind wandered.

"Are *you* the mousebug?" she whispered playfully.

The bug buzzed out the window and was gone. Sophie's eyes fixed on a patch of blue sky outside. It had been raining for days. Now the sun was finally poking through. She could just make out a pale misty rainbow.

The groundhog's rainbow! Sophie thought, smiling to herself.

Mrs. Wise dismissed the class for the day. "We'll talk more about legends on Monday!" she called as everyone stood up.

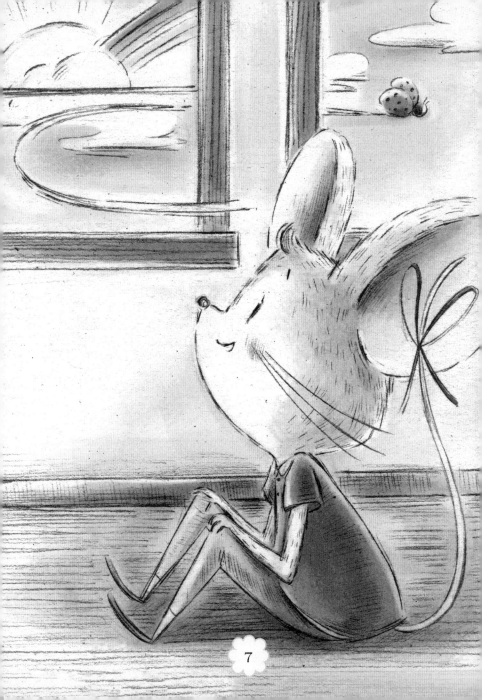

7

Sophie hurried outside to get a better look at the rainbow. At the foot of the steps, she stopped next to her friends Hattie Frog and Owen Snake.

"Look, you guys!" she said, pointing up at the sky.

But they didn't hear. They were listening to Ben, a rabbit, who was talking about something.

"Winston, check out the rainbow!" Sophie said to her little brother, who had come over. But he was listening to Ben too.

Sophie studied the rainbow. How could she paint one to look misty like that? *Start with pale colors,* she decided. *Then go over it with a wash of water to blend the colors.*

All the rainy days had kept Sophie from painting outside. With the weather clearing, she wanted to get back to it.

Sophie couldn't wait to paint—all weekend long!

chapter 2

A New Recipe

"See you on Sunday!" Sophie called to Hattie. The two friends were going to check out Rosebush Ravine. Owen already had plans, so he couldn't join.

Sophie grabbed Winston's hand. She pulled him toward home. "Let's get this weekend started!" Sophie exclaimed.

They ran along the path until a large oak tree came into view. At the base of the trunk, the mouse family's house was tucked between two roots.

Winston stopped in his tracks. He looked at Sophie with a sly smile. Then he called out, "Race you home!" Winston took off before the words were out of his mouth.

Sophie raced after him. She got to the oak tree first. Winston was only two steps behind her.

"I lost *again*," Winston said glumly. He kicked at a pine needle on the ground.

Sophie patted him on the back. "Yeah, but you're getting so much faster. We almost tied this time!"

Winston kicked at the pine needle again. But Sophie saw his whiskers twitch. He was trying not to smile.

Inside, George Mouse was hard at work at his drafting table. Mr. Mouse was an architect. At the moment, he was drawing up plans for a chipmunk family's lake home.

Sophie peeked over his shoulder. He had started with a blank piece of paper that morning. Now he had the outline of a whole house!

Winston ran in from the kitchen.
"We're out of bread," he told his dad.

"Can I go visit Mom at the bakery?" Lily Mouse owned the only bakery in Pine Needle Grove.

Mr. Mouse glanced up from his work. "If your sister will go with you."

Winston looked at Sophie with pleading eyes. Sophie's tummy rumbled. She *could* use an afternoon snack.

"Okay!" said Sophie. "Let's go!"

They scurried down the path to town. As they went, they played stone hop, one of their favorite games. They looked for stones or sticks along the path and hopped from one to the next. They went as far as they could without touching the ground.

At the bakery Lily Mouse was taking a tray out of the oven.

"Hello!" she cried when she saw them. "You're just in time! I need tasters for my newest recipe: clover-flower and almond scones."

Mrs. Mouse put a warm scone in each of their hands. Sophie blew on hers, then tasted it. "Yum!" she cried. "This is *good*." Her mom was always inventing new flavor combinations.

Sophie helped move the rest of the scones to a cooling rack.

"Do you remember my friend Clio?" Mrs. Mouse said.

Sophie nodded. Clio was a chipmunk who lived over in the Clover Patch.

"I was visiting her the other day," Mrs. Mouse went on. "The clovers were in full bloom. So I picked some. And I started to experiment!"

As she finished her scone, Sophie pictured the Clover Patch. In her

mind, she could see the pale lavender of the flowers and the bright green of the clover leaves.

Suddenly, Sophie had the urge to experiment too—with color!

The Clover Patch! That's where I'll go to paint tomorrow, she thought. *I can mix some new clover green paint right there on the spot!*

— chapter 3 —

Stop, Thief!

The next morning, after breakfast, Sophie packed up her things. She folded up her easel. She put paints, brushes, mixing jars, and a water canteen into her satchel. She tucked a pad of art paper under one arm.

It would be a lot to carry. But Sophie didn't have far to go. The Clover Patch was a short walk from her house.

She took the path toward the stream. She passed by Hattie's house. But Sophie knew Hattie couldn't come with her, so she didn't bother stopping in.

Halfway to Forget-Me-Not Lake,

Sophie turned off the path. She cut
across a meadow. On the other side,
she came to the edge of the Clover
Patch.

Bright green clovers stretched out
as far as Sophie could see. Perched

on top were purple pom-pom blooms. Sophie took a deep breath. The air was full of their sweet scent. She spotted a few red ladybugs hanging out on clover leaves.

Sophie found a good spot. She set up her easel. She pulled out a sheet of paper. She mixed up some colors.

She mixed raspberry red, blueberry blue, and wisteria white to make a beautiful pale purple. It was perfect for the clover flowers.

Poppy red plus a drop of bark brown would be good for painting the little ladybugs.

And Sophie would need lots of green! She picked a clover. She ground it into a powder. Then she took out her water canteen. She added a few drops to the powder. "Clover green!" she announced.

Sophie began to paint. She made the lines of the clover stems.

She formed the heart shapes of the

big leaves.

She dabbed on the pale purple. It made the clover flowers look fuzzy.

Sophie was lost in her work. She did not hear the bees buzzing by. She did not see the butterflies playing tag overhead. She barely felt the breeze on her fur.

Sophie also did not hear an animal rustling the clovers. Suddenly, a young chipmunk jumped out from his hiding place.

"Oh!" Sophie cried in surprise. "Hello!"

The chipmunk didn't answer. He stood beside Sophie's easel, flicking his tail. He put his nose up close to her painting. He looked at Sophie. He looked down at her paints.

Then, in a flash, he grabbed the

paintbrush from the jar of clover
green. He zipped away.

"Hey!" Sophie cried. "Stop!" She
dropped her other brush and chased
after him. "Come back here with my
paintbrush!"

chapter 4

Tea Time

Sophie sprinted, chasing the chipmunk to the far side of the Clover
Patch. He leaped out into a clearing,
then darted into a little grass hut. He
slammed the door behind him.

Sophie fumed. But she wasn't
about to give up! She marched up to
the door and knocked loudly.

Moments later, the door swung

open. Sophie opened her mouth to demand her paintbrush, but—

"Sophie!" cried the chipmunk staring back at her.

What? This wasn't the one she'd been chasing.

It was Clio, her mother's friend!

"Your mom didn't tell me you'd be stopping by," Clio said kindly.

"Well, I . . ." Sophie began. "I was just painting in the Clover Patch." She peered over Clio's shoulder. That little chipmunk had to be in there somewhere.

"Painting, you say?" Clio asked

curiously. "So the dripping wet paint-brush that my son Caleb just brought in . . ." Clio smiled apologetically at Sophie. "I bet that belongs to you?"

Sophie smiled and nodded.

"Caleb!" Clio called. Then she took Sophie by the hand. "Please, come in dear. I'm sorry about this. Caleb is only four. And we're still working on manners," she said with a wink.

The young chipmunk shuffled in from another room.

He had his hands behind his back.

"Caleb," said Clio, "this is my friend Sophie. I think you have something of hers?"

Caleb shook his head. "No, I don't," he replied with wide eyes.

Drip, drip. Drops of green paint splattered onto the floor behind Caleb's feet.

"Caleb . . ." said Clio firmly.

Caleb sighed.

"Sorry," he said

shyly, handing over the brush. Then his face brightened. "Can she stay for tea?" he asked Clio.

"Of course!" Clio replied, looking at Sophie. "If she'd like."

Sophie nodded. So Clio made a pot of clover tea. Meanwhile, Sophie had a chance to look around Clio's tidy little house. Nearly everything was shaped like a clover: the windows, the table, the stools, and even the teacups that Clio poured the tea into.

The three of them sat down at the table. Caleb reached for a clover-shaped biscuit. Clio and Sophie sipped their tea and chatted. Clio asked about the colorful paint smudges on Sophie's hands. Sophie explained how she'd made a new color from clover leaves.

"Clovers are such special plants,"

Clio said. "Animals come to pick them for so many uses—for dyes, for food, even for medicines."

After tea, Sophie thanked Clio. She said good-bye to Caleb and headed back to her easel. On the way, she plucked a few more clovers. She would need to make more clover green.

Sophie's eyes fell on a clover up ahead. It was the perfect shade of green. She reached out, grabbed the stem, and pulled.

Its leaves were so large!

No, that's not it, Sophie thought.

Then she gasped. "It's a four-leaf clover!" she cried. "What good luck!"

chapter 5

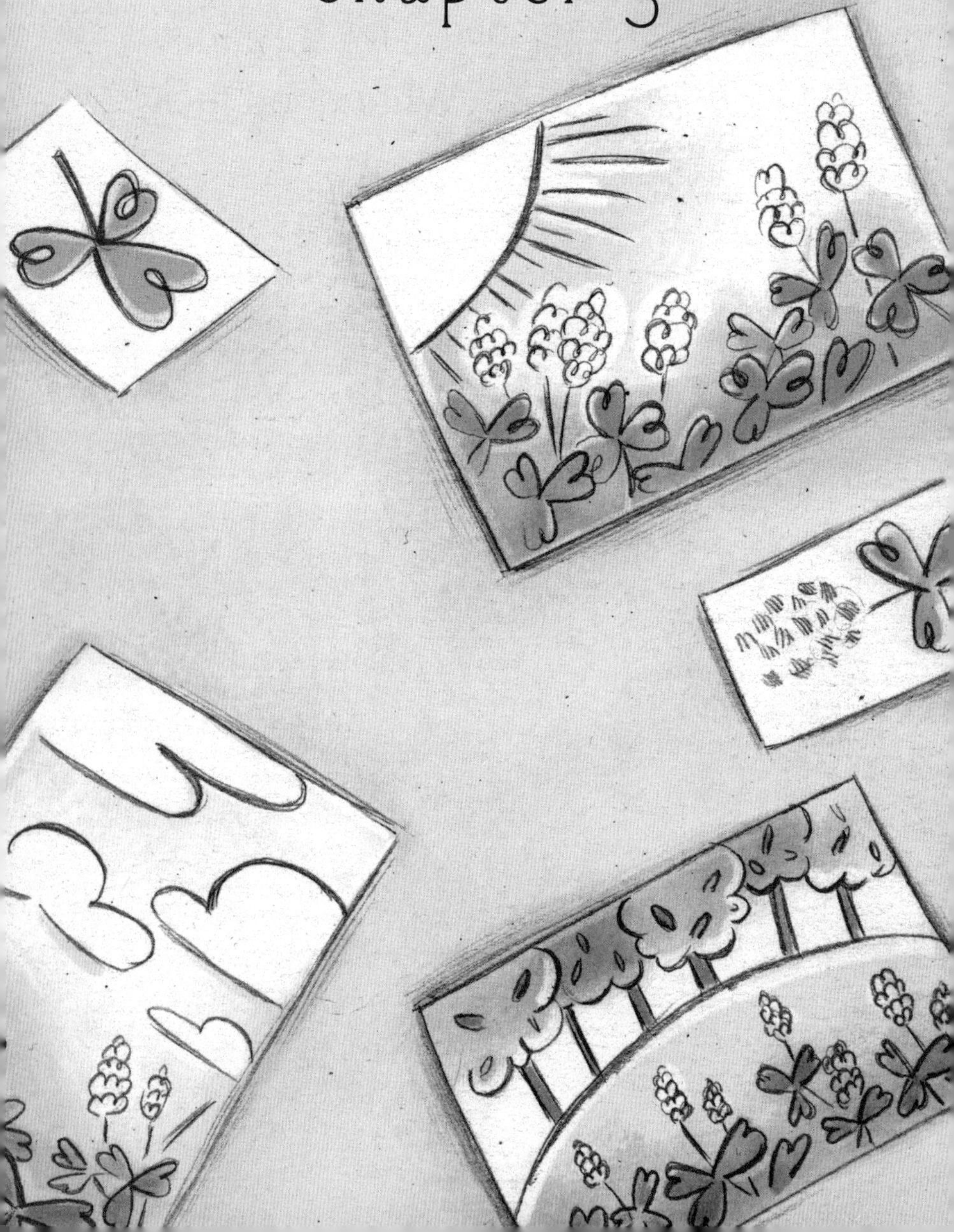

Rain, Rain, Go Away

Sophie painted the morning away. She painted three landscapes. Then she made some up-close studies of a clover leaf and a clover flower. She did a portrait of a bumblebee who was willing to sit still for a while.

Sophie had to make several batches of clover green paint. But she made sure not to grind up the

four-leaf clover! Sophie leaned it against her easel. She planned to carry it home carefully when it was time to go. That time came sooner than she expected. *Plip. Plop.* Two giant drops fell onto Sophie's latest painting.

Sophie gazed up. The sky was getting darker and darker. *That's odd,* she thought. *Usually I can smell the rain coming.* She shrugged. Maybe she'd been too wrapped up in her painting to notice.

All of Sophie's paintings were spread out on the ground to dry. She quickly tucked them inside her paper

pad. She threw paints and brushes into her satchel. She folded her easel. Finally, she grabbed the four-leaf clover. Then she started running for home.

She was barely out of the Clover Patch when it began to pour. Sophie groaned. Her paintings! She couldn't bear the thought of them getting soaked. As she ran, Sophie tried to

shield the papers with her satchel. But the rain was so heavy! Her heart sank further with each sloshy step.

Halfway home, Sophie stepped in some mud. Her feet slipped and she slid across the mud puddle. She was falling over backward! She threw her arms out to the side and caught herself. But a few paint tins fell out of her satchel. Sophie had to stop to pluck them out of the mud.

Meanwhile, the paper was getting wetter and wetter.

Finally, Sophie ran up the front path to her house. She dashed in

through the front door, slamming it
behind her.

Muddy and soaked, she stood
there catching her breath.

Mr. and Mrs. Mouse looked up from their reading. "Oh, sweetheart," her mom said sympathetically. "Got caught in the rain?"

Sophie nodded sadly. A lump was rising in her throat. She felt as if she was going to cry.

She dragged herself up the stairs to her room. She dropped her things and put her pad of paper down on her table. She took a deep breath. Then she opened the cover.

It was worse than she feared. All of her beautiful paintings! They were nothing but watery streaks of paint.

chapter 6

Winston's Weird Story

Sophie woke up the next morning feeling a little better. Though she was still sad about her paintings. She had put so much time and care into them.

At least I got one *good thing out of yesterday,* she thought.

Her four-leaf clover was in a vase by her window. She brought it down to breakfast. She wanted to show Winston.

"Look what I found yesterday!" Sophie said as she came down the stairs.

Winston took one look at the clover and nearly choked on his berries.

"Sophie!" he cried. "What are you doing with that?"

Sophie didn't understand. "I found it at the

Clover Patch," she said. "It'll bring me good luck!"

Winston shook his head. "No." His eyes were wide. "Didn't you hear Ben? At school?"

Sophie shook her head. "What are

you talking about, Winston?"

Winston sighed. "Sophie, why would you pick *that* clover when Ben told us all about the Clover Curse!"

Sophie thought back to Friday after school. She'd been studying the rainbow. Everyone else had been listening to Ben.

"A *four-leaf* clover curse?" Sophie said in disbelief. "Winston, that makes no sense. Everyone knows they're *good* luck."

Winston jumped up. "No really!" he cried. "That's what Ben said."

Sophie asked Winston for more
details. But he couldn't remember
much. "It's just . . . there was this animal . . . and there was this clover . . .
with *four leaves* . . . and then soon
after the animal picked it, he started
having bad luck!"

"Like what?" asked Sophie.

Winston couldn't remember. Sophie smiled. It didn't sound so convincing. But Sophie didn't feel like arguing, so she changed the subject.

"Want to go to the playground after breakfast?" she asked Winston.

Winston's face lit up. "Yeah!" he shouted. Just like that, the Clover Curse seemed forgotten.

At the playground, they were the only ones there. They played on the seesaw for a little while. Then they decided to race. Sophie expected to win as usual. She even let Winston be the one to say "go."

"Ready, set . . . go!" Winston cried. And he bolted off the starting line.

Sophie's back foot sank down into a pile of pine needles. She got a slow start. Halfway across the playground, she'd caught up to Winston. Then she ran into a cloud of gnats. One of them flew in her ear. She slowed as she tried to get it out.

Winston easily won. He cheered with excitement. "You were right!" he said. "I *am* getting faster!"

Sophie's shoulders slumped. *But if those gnats hadn't been in my way* . . . she thought. She probably could have won.

A little later, two friends from school showed up: Malcolm, a mole, and Piper, a hummingbird. Winston was swinging on the swing. Sophie sat at the top of the jungle gym with Piper and Malcolm.

"Hey," Sophie said uncertainly. "Did you guys hear Ben telling some clover story on Friday? After school?"

Malcolm and Piper looked puzzled. "What clover story?" Piper asked.

Sophie couldn't believe she'd even asked. "Never mind," she said.

chapter 7

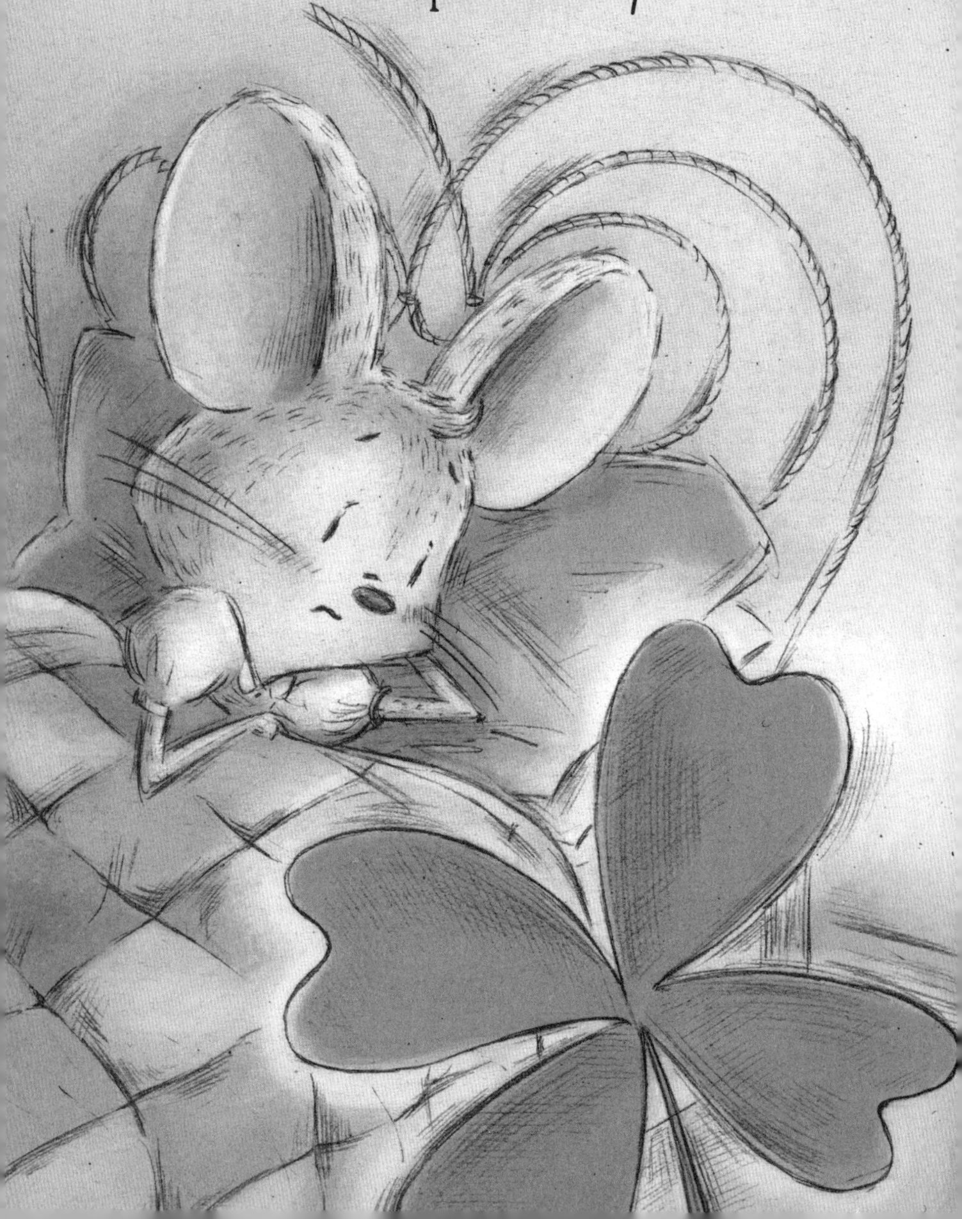

coincidence or curse?

That night Sophie lay in bed, staring at the four-leaf clover.

Okay, it was true. She'd had some bad luck over the weekend. She'd lost her race with Winston at the playground. Then Malcolm and Piper had invited them along to visit Zoe. On the way, Sophie had tripped and scraped her knee. *And getting caught in the rain* . . . thought Sophie. She winced. It was still hard to look at her ruined paintings.

Sophie was doubtful about the Clover Curse. Winston must have gotten it wrong somehow. But maybe she'd ask Ben about it at school anyway.

The next morning Sophie woke up late. At breakfast she spilled tea all over her jumper. She rushed upstairs to change. Then, while

brushing her teeth, she didn't notice
a hole in the sink pipe. Water sprayed
everywhere, soaking Sophie. Sophie
ran off to change her clothes *again*.

Hurrying out the door, she
grabbed her satchel—upside-down.

Everything spilled onto the floor. She threw it all back in as fast as she could.

Of course, Sophie and Winston were late to school. Mrs. Wise eyed them sternly as they walked in. Sophie hated how everyone turned to look. She and Winston made their way to their desks.

Sophie slumped into her seat. She glanced over at Hattie.

The look on Hattie's face said, "Everything okay?"

Sophie responded with a look that said, "Don't ask."

And now I'll have to wait until recess to ask Ben about the Clover Curse! Sophie realized. She glanced over at Ben's desk.

It was empty!

Where was Ben?

The morning seemed to drag on and on. Finally, Mrs. Wise dismissed the class for recess. Sophie practically jumped out of her seat. She hurried outside.

"James!" Sophie called to Ben's little brother. "Is Ben out sick?"

James nodded. "He's all stuffed up," he said. "Maybe allergies."

Hattie and Owen came over. "Hi," Hattie said gently. "Rough morning?"

Sophie snorted. "Rough *week-end!*" she said. She told her friends about her string of bad luck. "But it started off so well! On Saturday, I went to paint in the Clover Patch. I made a bunch of paintings I really liked." She sighed. "I even found a four-leaf clover and I—"

Owen and Hattie gasped loudly together.

"Oh no!" cried Owen. "The Clover Curse!"

"You didn't pick it, did you?" Hattie asked.

"That's exactly what Winston said!" Sophie replied. "I didn't hear

Ben talking about it."

Obviously, Hattie and Owen had!

Sophie looked at her friends doubtfully. "It can't be for real," she said. "Can it?"

"Well . . . you did forget about the trip we had planned to Rosebush Ravine," Hattie said quietly.

Sophie's hands flew up to her mouth in shock. How could she have forgotten about Hattie?! And they had both been so excited about exploring Rosebush Ravine, too!

"I'm so sorry Hattie," Sophie said sincerely.

"It's okay," replied Hattie. She patted Sophie on the back. "Just some bad luck, I guess!"

— chapter 8 —

Sophie Gives Up

Hattie and Owen told Sophie every-thing they remembered from Ben's story.

"The thing is," said Hattie, "it didn't sound like just a story."

"Ben said his grandfather once found a four-leaf clover," explained Owen. "Right afterward, he started having terrible luck."

Hattie nodded. "Until the grandfather tossed the clover into a river.
It floated away, along with his bad
luck."

Sophie groaned. Now she *really*
wanted to talk to Ben.

"Oh, why did he have to be sick
today?" she cried.

For the rest of the day, Sophie

tried to be so careful. It was no use.

She bumped into the side
of Mrs. Wise's desk.
A mug toppled off
and smashed.

"Don't worry,"
Mrs. Wise said kindly.
"It was an accident." But Sophie
felt terrible.

Then, on the walk home, a sour cherry dropped from a tree. It landed right on Sophie's head. Not only did it *hurt*, now Sophie had cherry juice all over her!

She got home and cleaned herself up. But the sour cherry juice had left a stain. Lily Mouse took a look and shook her head. "Sour cherry juice is hard to get out," she said. "It will fade in a few days."

That's when Sophie's frustration bubbled over. The clover had to go. Curse or no curse, she *had* to try something.

She grabbed the four-leaf clover from her room. She headed for the stream, stopping to get Hattie on the way.

They stood on the bank, side by side. Sophie lifted the clover over her head. She got ready to throw it in.

She hesitated. She had never found a four-leaf clover before in her whole life! Now here she was, about to toss it away.

"On the count of three," Hattie said.

Sophie carefully stepped out onto a thin branch that hung over the water. She looked back at Hattie on the stream bank.

"One, two, three!"

She threw the clover. It floated downstream.

Sophie and Hattie watched it until they couldn't see it anymore.

"Well," said Sophie. "That's the end of that."

Crrrrrack!

At that very moment, the branch broke under Sophie's weight. The end splashed down into the shallow water, taking Sophie with it.

Sophie stood up, soaked to her neck. She looked at Hattie.

"Oh no," she moaned. "Am I cursed . . . *forever*?"

— chapter 9 —

Ben Returns

The next morning part of Sophie felt like staying in bed all day. How could bad luck strike if she stayed under her covers?

But the other part of her wanted to get to school early. She had to talk to Ben!

So Sophie got out of bed very carefully. She clutched the handrail extra tight as she went downstairs to breakfast.

She gasped at every clink of dishes, thinking she had knocked something over.

On the way to school, she heard a rustle in the trees above. She dove off the path and took cover.

"It's okay," Winston reported. "Just a couple of squirrels."

Sophie figured she couldn't be too careful. Bad luck could be waiting at every turn.

She and Winston got to school with a few minutes to spare.

Mrs. Wise was still unpacking her tote bag. Sophie scanned the room. She waved at Hattie and Owen. Lydie, Malcolm, Piper, Zoe, and Willy were already there too.

Not Ben. Sophie's heart fell. *Where is he?* she thought. Sophie didn't want to wait until recess to ask him about the Clover Curse. Then she had a worse thought: *What if he's absent again!*

Too soon, Mrs. Wise asked everyone to sit down. Sophie sighed and dragged herself to her desk.

Just as she sat, the door flew open. James came hurrying in. Right behind him was Ben!

"Just in time," Mrs. Wise said to them.

Ben and James sat down as Mrs. Wise began the lesson.

"We're going to talk more about legends this morning," she said. "Did any of you think of others over the weekend?"

The room was quiet. Mrs. Wise waited patiently.

Suddenly, Sophie had an idea. This was her chance! Her hand flew up. Mrs. Wise called on her.

"I heard a story over the weekend," Sophie said. "It's something about a Clover Curse?"

Sophie watched Ben's reaction. His eyes went wide and he turned to look at her. Hattie, Owen, and Winston did too.

Mrs. Wise tapped her chin. "I haven't heard that one," she said. "Has anyone else?"

Slowly, Ben raised his hand. "I have," he said.

"Would you tell us about it?" asked Mrs. Wise.

Sophie smiled. *Yes!* she thought. *Now I don't have to wait until recess for more details!*

"W-Well," Ben said. "I mean . . ." He seemed unsure how to begin. "It's a story about my grandfather. . . ." His voice trailed off.

"Oh! How interesting!" Mrs. Wise said. "Just tell the version you know. We can see how it compares to what Sophie heard."

So Ben told the story—the exact same story that Sophie had heard from Hattie, Owen, and Winston. He even included the part about the bad luck floating away along with the clover.

When he finished, Mrs. Wise

nodded. "Thank you Ben!"

"But Mrs. Wise," Ben said. "There's one more thing. I know for sure that legend is *not* true."

Sophie jumped in her seat.

"Aha!" Mrs. Wise replied. "How do you know?"

Sophie held her breath, eager to hear Ben's answer.

"I know," he said, "because I made that story up."

— chapter 10 —

Good-Luck charm

Ben explained that he and Willy had been playing a game on Friday after school. "We were making up different legends and tales," Ben said.

Mrs. Wise started to pass out paper. "How funny," she said. "Because that's our writing assignment today! Each of you is going to write a legend."

Sophie's mind was spinning. She was full of questions! There was no such thing as a Clover Curse? Then why did she have such bad luck?

At recess, she bolted out the door. She made a beeline for Ben and Willy. Hattie and Owen were right on Sophie's heels.

Sophie caught up to Ben. "So there's really no Legend of the Clover Curse?" she asked him, out of breath.

Ben shook his head. "Did you think there was?" he asked.

Hattie spoke up. "Well, *I* did . . . sort of. I was listening on Friday."

Owen poked his head between

them. "Yeah. Why didn't you say it was just made up?"

"You must have missed the beginning," Ben said. "Willy challenged me to think something up on the spot." Ben looked apologetic. "I wasn't trying to fool you or anything."

Hattie and Owen looked sheep-ishly at Sophie.

"Sorry Sophie," said Owen. "I guess we made you worry for no reason."

Sophie smiled. "That's okay," she said. She pulled at her whiskers. "But I just don't get it. There's no Clover Curse. So why has everything been going wrong for me lately?"

Owen shrugged.

"Maybe just a really bad

weekend?" Hattie suggested.

Sophie smiled. Then she started to laugh. "Really, *really* bad!"

Sophie felt so relieved. She wasn't cursed after all! And surely her luck was about to change.

That day, after school, Sophie
grabbed her painting supplies. She
headed back to the Clover Patch. This
time, there wasn't a cloud in the sky
or a drop of rain. And her paintings

turned out even better than the first batch.

As she finished the last one, Sophie felt a pang of regret. *Too bad I threw away that four-leaf clover,* she thought. *But I'm sure I'll find another.*

In the meantime, she could paint herself a good-luck charm.

The End

Here's a peek at the next
Adventures of Sophie Mouse book!

the adventures of   8

SOPHIE MOUSE

A surprise visitor

— by Poppy Green • illustrated by Jennifer A. Bell —

 One day Sophie Mouse is startled by a noise outside her home. When she peeks outside, she's surprised to see that a little bird has made a crash landing into her yard! And it turns out he's hurt his wing. Can Sophie help fix his wing so he can return home?

the adventures of
SOPHiE MOUSE

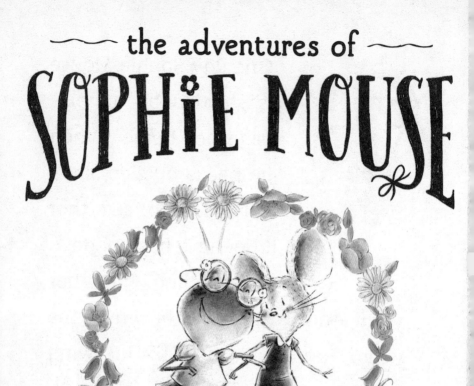

For excerpts, activities, and more about these adorable tales & tails, visit AdventuresofSophieMouse.com!